CONTAGION

A Thrilling Crime Mystery

ARIEL SANDERS

Index

SPECIAL BONUS

*Want this Bonus Ebook for **free**?*

SCAN ME

SCAN W/ YOUR CAMERA TO DOWNLOAD THE EBOOK!

PART I
ARCTIC SHADOW

The wind howled across the ice, a mournful wail that seemed to warn against trespassing in this desolate corner of the Arctic. Dr. Elara Voss pressed her forehead against the helicopter window, watching the endless white expanse glide beneath them. Three years here, and she still couldn't get used to the isolation. The landscape was beautiful in its stark emptiness—pristine, untouched. Perfect for hiding things the world wasn't ready to see.

"Five minutes to touchdown, Dr. Voss," the pilot announced through her headset.

She nodded, though she knew he couldn't see her. As the helicopter banked, Elara caught a glimpse of their destination: nothing but a small cluster of prefabricated structures dotting the ice like gray scabs on white skin. The visible portion was merely administrative—a facade. The real facility, Research Station Polaris, lay beneath, carved into the ancient rock of the mountain range.

The chopper landed with a gentle bump. Elara gathered her tablet and research notes, zipped her thermal coat to her chin, and disembarked. The biting cold stole her breath immediately. At minus forty, the air itself felt brittle, as if it might shatter.

Colonel Nathan Mercer waited for her at the entrance to the main building, standing rigid and unaffected by the cold. His military posture never wavered, even here, thousands of miles from any formal review. His face was weathered by years of service, eyes sharp beneath salt-and-pepper brows.

"Welcome back, Doctor. Productive trip to the mainland?" His voice was clipped, professional.

"Very," she replied, stepping through the door he held open. "The protein synthesis modifications show promise. I have the models ready for your review."

Mercer nodded curtly and walked beside her down the sterile corridor. Their footsteps echoed on the polished concrete floor. "The brass is getting impatient. General Harwick called twice this week."

Elara felt her shoulders tense. "Science doesn't operate on military timetables, Colonel."

"When the DoD funds your science, Doctor, it does."

They reached the elevator—a reinforced steel cage that would take them down to the real Polaris. Mercer pressed his palm against the scanner, then leaned forward for a retinal scan. The doors slid open with a soft pneumatic hiss.

"How's Reyes doing?" Elara asked as they descended.

A hint of a smile crossed Mercer's face. "Subject R-9 is exceeding expectations. Physical endurance at 97%. Cognitive function optimal. He's everything the program promised."

Elara said nothing. Subject R-9, whom the staff had nicknamed "Reyes," was the pride of Mercer's Prometheus Unit—elite soldiers subjected to experimental medical treatments designed to enhance their natural abilities. Enhanced immune systems, increased endurance, accelerated healing—the perfect soldiers to field-test what her research would eventually deliver. The thought left a sour taste in her mouth.

The elevator stopped with a gentle lurch, five hundred meters below the surface. When the doors opened, they revealed a different world—bright, immaculate, humming with purpose. Lab techs in white coats moved efficiently between workstations. Armed guards stood at strategic points, faces impassive.

"Dr. Takeda was asking for you," Mercer said. "Something about unexpected viral behavior."

Elara felt a flutter of concern. "I'll head to his lab now."

"Keep me updated," Mercer said, already turning toward the command center. "And Voss? Remember—we're making history here. A virus that can selectively target and modify human immune response could change medicine forever. Not to mention warfare."

That's what I'm afraid of, she thought, but simply nodded.

Dr. Jin Takeda's virology lab was at the far end of the main corridor. Elara found him hunched over a digital microscope, his lean frame curved like a question mark. At forty-two, Jin's temples were already graying, the price of brilliance and stress in equal measure.

"Jin," she called softly.

He straightened immediately, relief washing over his face. "Elara, thank God. Come look at this."

She crossed to his workstation, setting down her things. "Mercer said something about unexpected behavior?"

"That's putting it mildly." Jin pulled up a time-lapse on his screen. "This is XV-27 three weeks ago, batch 37." The display showed a standard viral structure, one they'd engineered over countless iterations. "And this is the same batch today."

The changes were subtle but unmistakable to a trained eye. The protein coat had restructured, the RNA sequences subtly reordered.

"That's impossible," Elara whispered. "The stabilization matrix should prevent drift beyond 0.02%."

"It's showing 3.7% deviation. And look—" Jin swiped to another screen. "The changes aren't random. They're targeted, focusing on transmission vectors."

A chill that had nothing to do with the Arctic location crawled up Elara's spine. "We designed it to be injection-only. Non-communicable."

"Not anymore," Jin said quietly. "Simulation models suggest it's one, maybe two mutations away from airborne capability."

Elara leaned heavily against the lab bench. XV-27 was already the most sophisticated viral agent ever created—designed to "prep" human physiology for enhancement by temporarily rewriting specific immune responses without killing the host. If it could self-modify its transmission methods...

"We need to pause the trials," she said. "This is beyond our safety protocols."

Jin's laugh was hollow. "Try telling that to Mercer. The Prometheus Unit trials are scheduled for tomorrow. First live human deployment after the chimps."

"That's insane! We haven't even characterized these mutations!"

"Funding deadlines," Jin said with resignation. "The military wants results, not caution."

Elara straightened her shoulders. "I'm going to talk to him."

"Good luck with that," Jin muttered, turning back to his work. "Just... be careful, Elara. Mercer sees obstacles, not people."

Elara found Colonel Mercer in the command center, surrounded by holographic displays of the facility's systems. Military personnel moved efficiently around him, preparing for tomorrow's demonstration. The colonel was studying test subject data, his face illuminated by the blue glow of the screen.

She took a deep breath and approached. "Colonel, we need to talk. Privately."

Mercer glanced up, his expression hardening slightly at her tone. "I'm rather busy, Doctor."

"It's about XV-27. It's urgent."

Something in her voice must have registered because Mercer nodded curtly and gestured toward a glass-walled conference room adjacent to the command center. Once inside, he pressed a button that frosted the glass, giving them privacy.

"What's so urgent it couldn't wait until the briefing?" he asked, remaining standing, arms crossed.

Elara placed her tablet on the table, displaying Jin's data. "The virus is mutating at an unprecedented rate. The stabilization matrix we engineered is failing."

"Failing how, exactly?"

"It's showing a 3.7% drift from baseline—nearly twenty times what should be possible. And the mutations aren't random. They're concentrated in the transmission vectors."

Mercer leaned over the tablet, his brow furrowing. "Meaning?"

"Meaning it's evolving toward airborne transmission. We designed it to be injection-only, specifically to prevent uncontrolled spread. If these mutations continue..." She let the implication hang in the air.

"How certain are you of this analysis?"

"Jin ran the models three times. The trend is clear."

Mercer straightened, his jaw set. "And what exactly are you proposing, Doctor?"

"We need to postpone tomorrow's trials. At minimum, we need to characterize these mutations fully before proceeding with human testing. The risk—"

"The risk," Mercer interrupted, "is acceptable."

Elara stared at him in disbelief. "Acceptable? Colonel, we're talking about a potential containment breach. If XV-27 goes airborne during the trial—"

"Our containment protocols are the best in the world. The testing chamber is designed to handle pathogens far more contagious than anything we've engineered."

"That's my point," Elara insisted. "We didn't engineer this. The virus is engineering itself now, finding ways around our safeguards. We need time to understand what's happening."

Mercer's eyes narrowed. "What we need, Doctor, is results. Six generals and three undersecretaries are flying in specifically for tomorrow's demonstration. Billions in future funding depends on what they see."

"And if what they see is a containment failure? Or worse, if what they don't see is that we've released an airborne pathogen that could—"

"That's enough." Mercer's voice was ice. "You're catastrophizing, Doctor Voss. Your concern is noted, but the trial proceeds as scheduled."

Elara felt her temper rising. "This isn't about hitting project milestones or impressing the brass. This is about basic scientific responsibility. We created this virus—"

"That's right, you did," Mercer cut in. "Under military contract, with military objectives. XV-27 isn't some academic curiosity; it's a strategic asset years in development. We don't pause strategic deployment because of theoretical concerns."

"They're not theoretical. The data clearly shows—"

"The data shows a virus doing exactly what it was designed to do: adapt to maximize effectiveness." Mercer leaned forward, placing his palms flat on the table. "That's the whole point of the Prometheus Project, Doctor. Creating agents that can overcome enemy countermeasures in real-time."

Elara shook her head. "We designed it to adapt within controlled parameters, to enhance the host without causing systemic damage. What it's doing now is something else entirely."

"Or it's evolving faster than your models predicted. That's called exceeding expectations, and in my world, it's a good thing."

She tried a different approach. "Just give us seventy-two hours. Three days to run additional tests, create better containment protocols. The demonstration will be more impressive with complete data."

For a moment, Mercer seemed to consider this. Then he shook his head. "The schedule stands. Reyes has been prepped, the observers are en route, and frankly, Doctor, your overcaution is noted in your file."

The implied threat wasn't subtle. Push too hard, and her role in the project could be reconsidered.

"Are you genuinely willing to risk an uncontained outbreak to meet a deadline?" she asked quietly.

Mercer straightened, his military bearing impossibly rigid. "What I'm willing to do, Doctor Voss, is trust our systems, trust our protocols, and trust that the brilliant scientist who created XV-27 built in enough safeguards to prevent the nightmare scenario you're so fond of imagining."

He moved toward the door, conversation clearly over in his mind. "The trial proceeds at 0900 tomorrow. I expect your full cooperation and professionalism in front of our visitors. Is that understood?"

Elara stood her ground. "And if I refuse to participate?"

Mercer turned, his expression cold but not entirely without sympathy. "Then you'll miss witnessing the culmination of your life's work, and your replacement will receive credit for the breakthrough. The military appreciates your contributions, Doctor Voss, but no one person is indispensable to the mission."

He paused at the door. "I suggest you get some rest. Tomorrow will be a historic day for medicine and modern warfare. Be proud of what you've accomplished."

With that, he was gone, leaving Elara alone with the knowledge that tomorrow would indeed be historic—but perhaps not in the way Mercer imagined.

She gathered her tablet and composed herself. There was work to do. If she couldn't stop the trial, she could at least prepare for the worst. She needed to find Jin and begin emergency planning.

As she left the conference room, the lights flickered briefly—a minor power fluctuation common in facilities this remote. But in that moment, it felt ominous, as if the very infrastructure of Polaris was trembling at what was to come.

PART II
CONTAINMENT BREACH

The observation chamber above Testing Lab 3 was crowded the next morning. Various military officials had flown in for the demonstration, along with the project's key scientists. The air smelled of expensive cologne and coffee, overlaid with the sterile scent of industrial disinfectant. The low hum of conversation ceased as Mercer entered, followed by three generals whose chests sagged with decorations.

Elara stood with Jin near the back, anxiety gnawing at her. She hadn't slept—how could she? The statistical models she'd run all night only confirmed her fears: XV-27 was evolving beyond their control. She'd tried one last email to Mercer at 4 AM, with all the new data. His one-line response: "Proceed as scheduled."

Jin leaned close. "I loaded a rapid-response antiviral into the emergency system," he whispered. "Not that I expect it to work, but..."

She nodded gratefully. At least someone else recognized the danger.

Below, through the reinforced glass, Subject R-9—Reyes—sat calmly on an examination table. Unlike the other test subjects who were kept sedated between trials, Reyes had full consciousness and autonomy within limits. His physical conditioning was already impressive: increased muscle density, enhanced reflexes, accelerated healing from previous conventional treatments. He was the perfect specimen to receive XV-27.

But something about him seemed off today. Maybe it was Elara's heightened state of anxiety, but his eyes seemed too alert, too calculating as they scanned the testing chamber. This wasn't the usual military detachment she'd observed in previous sessions. Something more predatory lurked behind his gaze.

A technician approached him with a small tray of monitoring devices—subdermal sensors to track his physiological responses during the test. As she applied them, Reyes tracked her movements with unusual intensity, his head tilting slightly, like a wolf assessing potential prey.

"Is he usually this... focused?" Elara whispered to Jin.

"No," Jin replied quietly. "His baseline neurological profile shows typical military compartmentalization. This is different."

Before she could respond, Mercer stepped to the microphone. The chamber fell silent.

"Gentlemen," he began, voice resonating with practiced authority, "what you're about to witness is the culmination of Project Prometheus. The fusion of cutting-edge viral engineering with elite military training. XV-27 will temporarily rewrite specific portions of Subject R-9's immune system, allowing for unprecedented physical performance, environmental adaptability, and resistance to known biological weapons."

A murmur of approval rippled through the assembled brass.

"In simpler terms," Mercer continued, casting a practiced smile toward the visitors, "we're creating the soldier of tomorrow. Immune to chemical attacks, capable of operating in any environment from Arctic ice to desert heat without acclimatization, and able to push the boundaries of human performance far beyond current limitations."

Elara exchanged glances with Jin. Neither spoke, but their shared concern was palpable. Mercer was overselling, making promises the science couldn't yet support—especially given the virus's unexpected mutations.

"Proceed," Mercer ordered, nodding to the team below.

The test chamber hummed with activity as final preparations were made. Monitors displayed Reyes's baseline vitals—heart rate slightly elevated but within normal parameters, blood pressure optimal, neural activity consistent with focused attention. A medical technician approached Reyes with a syringe. The clear fluid inside caught the light—XV-27, the culmination of years of research, now potentially their greatest threat.

Elara's mouth went dry. She wanted to scream, to stop this madness, but knew it would be futile. All she could do was watch and be ready to respond when—not if—things went wrong.

Reyes didn't flinch as the needle entered his arm, the viscous fluid disappearing into his bloodstream. For a moment, nothing happened. The monitors continued their steady display of normal function. Reyes remained still, expression neutral.

Then his body went rigid, back arching slightly. The vital signs displayed on the overhead monitors fluctuated wildly—heart rate spiking to 180, blood pressure surging, brain activity erupting across multiple regions simultaneously. Reyes's hands gripped the edges of the examination table, the metal actually bending under his fingers.

"Initial systemic shock," a technician announced, voice remarkably calm given the chaos on the monitors. "Expected response. Administering stabilizer."

A second technician quickly injected a clear fluid into Reyes's other arm—a buffering agent designed to moderate the virus's initial impact. Gradually, the wild fluctuations on the monitors began to settle.

"Vitals normalizing," the technician reported. "Primary integration phase complete."

Minutes passed. The tension in the room was palpable. Elara could hear the controlled breathing of the military men around her, the soft beep of the monitors, the almost imperceptible hum of the facility's air filtration system. Everyone was waiting, watching.

Then Reyes opened his eyes.

Elara felt a chill run through her. Something was different. His pupils were dilated, almost swallowing the iris, and his gaze had an unnerving intensity as it swept across the testing chamber. When he sat up, the movement was too smooth, too controlled—like a predator uncoiling.

"Cognitive assessment beginning," announced another technician.

A series of complex problems flashed on a screen before Reyes—mathematical equations, spatial reasoning puzzles, logical sequences. He solved them with increasing speed, his response times dropping with each new challenge. By the fifth problem, he was answering before the equations were fully displayed.

"Cognitive processing improved by 32% and climbing," the technician reported, unable to keep a note of awe from his voice. "Neural pathways showing unprecedented efficiency."

"What about inhibitory function?" Elara asked suddenly, unable to remain silent any longer.

The lead technician glanced at the relevant monitors. "Frontal lobe activity is... unusual. Elevated in some regions, suppressed in others."

"Be specific," she pressed.

"Areas associated with impulse control are showing decreased activity," the technician admitted. "But that's consistent with combat optimization—reducing hesitation in tactical scenarios."

Or removing the neurological brakes on aggression, Elara thought grimly.

Next came physical tests. Reyes stepped off the examination table, rolling his shoulders as if testing new equipment. He approached the physical testing area where weights and various exercise equipment had been arranged. The demonstration began with simple assessments—grip strength, standing jump, basic speed tests.

Reyes shattered every baseline. His grip crushed the dynamometer, maxing out its measurement capacity. His standing vertical leap cleared two meters easily. During the sprint test, the treadmill's motor burned out trying to match his pace.

The military observers were openly amazed now, nudging each other and pointing. One general clapped Mercer on the shoulder in congratulation. "Incredible," Elara heard him murmur. "Absolutely incredible."

As the physical demonstration continued, Reyes moved to more complex tests—an obstacle course designed to measure agility, coordination, and problem-solving under physical stress. His movements became a blur, his strength visibly increasing with each challenge. He didn't just complete the course; he demolished it, tearing through barriers that should have required tools to dismantle.

"Physical capability increased by 47%," reported the monitoring technician. "All vital signs stable."

Mercer was beaming. "As you can see, gentlemen, Project Prometheus has delivered as promised. This is just the beginning. Imagine a full unit of soldiers with these capabilities. The strategic implications are—"

A sharp crack interrupted him. Below, Reyes had snapped a solid steel bar in half without apparent effort. He stood examining the broken pieces with an expression of mild curiosity.

"Impressive demonstration of enhanced strength," Mercer recovered smoothly. "Our estimates suggest peak force output at approximately triple normal human maximum."

But Elara wasn't sharing in the celebration. Something in Reyes's demeanor bothered her deeply. Behind the impressive performance, his eyes seemed... different. Unfocused one moment, hyperfocused the next. He would stare at nothing for several seconds, then snap his attention to a specific point with unnerving intensity.

And his expression was changing. The disciplined neutrality of a trained soldier was eroding, replaced by micro-expressions that flashed across his face too quickly to fully register—flickers of confusion, dawning realization, and something that looked unsettlingly like pleasure.

The demonstration continued for another hour. Complex problem-solving, environmental adaptation tests, simulated combat scenarios—with each test, Reyes exceeded all projections. But as the session wore on, Elara noticed more disturbing changes in his behavior. Micro-expressions that didn't match the situation. Brief pauses where there should be none. A strange tilt to his head when addressed directly, as if he were listening to something no one else could hear.

Most concerning was his growing disregard for protocol. When instructed to wait between test segments, he simply proceeded at his own pace. When a technician attempted to apply additional monitoring sensors, Reyes brushed the man's hands away with casual strength that left bruises.

"Something's wrong," she whispered to Jin, who was studying the neural activity displays with growing alarm.

"I see it too," he confirmed, pointing to patterns on the screen. "Neurological markers are showing unusual patterns. The limbic system is hyperactive, especially the amygdala, while prefrontal activity is becoming erratic. Almost like—"

A crash from below interrupted him. Reyes had suddenly seized one of the monitoring devices—a complex piece of equipment worth millions—and smashed it against the wall with casual violence. Glass and circuitry exploded across the laboratory in a glittering spray.

The room above fell silent, the earlier congratulatory atmosphere evaporating instantly. Before anyone could react, Reyes had grabbed a technician by the throat, lifting the man off his feet with one hand. The technician's face reddened, his legs kicking uselessly as he struggled for air.

"Restrain the subject!" Mercer ordered into the microphone, all smugness gone from his voice.

Security personnel rushed forward, armed with stun batons designed to incapacitate even enhanced individuals. But Reyes moved with uncanny speed. He threw the technician into them like a rag doll, knocking three men down in a tangle of limbs. The technician's head hit the floor with a sickening crack, blood pooling instantly.

"My God," someone whispered behind Elara.

In seconds, Reyes had crossed the lab and was pounding on the reinforced door, the metal actually denting under his enhanced strength. Each impact echoed through the observation room like a thunderclap.

"Containment breach!" someone shouted. Alarms began blaring throughout the facility, red warning lights casting everything in a bloody glow.

The military observers were backing away from the window now, some reaching instinctively for sidearms that had been checked at security. Mercer remained at the control panel, face pale but composed as he activated emergency protocols.

"Flood the chamber with sedative gas," he ordered, his earlier smugness replaced by military efficiency.

White vapor poured from vents in the ceiling of the test lab, quickly filling the space with a chemical fog designed to render even the largest subjects unconscious within seconds. Reyes paused, his assault on the door temporarily halted as he noticed the changing environment.

For a moment, hope flickered in the observation room. Then, to everyone's horror, Reyes smiled—a cold, feral expression that transformed his face into something barely human—and continued his methodical assault on the door, each blow more powerful than the last.

"The gas isn't working," a technician reported, panic edging into his voice as he studied the monitors. "His system is metabolizing the compounds too quickly. It's like his liver function has increased exponentially."

"Increase concentration, maximum dose," Mercer commanded, fingers flying over the control panel.

More gas flooded the chamber, the white fog so thick now that Reyes was barely visible through it. The concentration was lethal to normal humans—enough to stop the heart and respiratory function within minutes. Reyes should have been unconscious on the floor.

Instead, the pounding continued, the door beginning to buckle under his enhanced strength. Through gaps in the fog, they could see him working methodically, targeting structural weak points with disturbing precision.

"He's going to break through," one of the generals said, voice tight with controlled fear. "What the hell is Plan B, Mercer?"

"Implement electrical countermeasures," Mercer ordered, ignoring the question as he activated another emergency system.

The floor of the testing chamber electrified, blue arcs of current racing across the metal surface. Reyes jerked as the current surged through him, a howl of pain escaping his lips as his muscles contracted involuntarily. He collapsed to his knees, body twitching as electricity coursed through him—enough voltage to kill an unmodified human instantly.

For a moment, it seemed the crisis had passed. Reyes remained on his knees, head bowed, apparently subdued. A collective sigh of relief passed through the observation room.

Then, slowly, demonstrating unbelievable control, he pushed himself back to his feet. The movement was unnatural, jerky, as if he were manipulating his own body like a puppet. His skin had taken on a grayish pallor, blue veins standing out in stark relief. Blood trickled from his nose and ears, yet he seemed completely unaware of it.

Looking directly at the observation window, he spoke his first words since the procedure: "I can feel it... changing me. I can feel... everything." His voice had a strange, unfamiliar quality, as if he were struggling to form the words, the cadence wrong, too slow in some places and too rapid in others.

"What the hell does that mean?" one of the generals demanded, backing further from the glass.

Elara felt sick, a cold sweat breaking out across her skin as understanding dawned. "The neurotropic component of XV-27... it was designed to temporarily enhance neural plasticity for better reflexes, but—"

"It's affecting his brain chemistry more profoundly than anticipated," Jin finished for her, face pale as he studied the neural readings. "The virus is crossing the blood-brain barrier and altering neurotransmitter production. Look at these patterns—it's completely rewiring his limbic system while suppressing frontal lobe function."

"In English, Doctor," Mercer snapped.

"It's enhancing instinct, aggression, and physical capability while suppressing impulse control, moral reasoning, and higher cognitive functions," Elara explained, her voice steady despite the terror clawing at her chest. "It's creating a perfect predator."

Below, Reyes had stopped attacking the door. Instead, he stood perfectly still, head tilted as if listening to something no one else could hear. His eyes roamed the room slowly, methodically, like a scanner mapping his environment. Then they fixed again on the observation window, and Elara could have sworn he was looking directly at her, despite the one-way glass.

A trickle of blood ran from his eye, cutting a crimson path down his cheek like a tear. Then another. And another.

His body began to twitch, subtle at first, then more violently. His back arched at an impossible angle, spine contorting as if something inside him was trying to break free. Blood now poured freely from his nose, eyes, and ears, pooling on the floor around him.

"He's hemorrhaging," Jin reported, studying the medical readouts. "Blood pressure spiking beyond measurable limits. Massive neurological cascade failure initiating."

"Is he dying?" Mercer asked tersely.

Jin shook his head, expression bewildered. "No, that's the thing—his vitals should be incompatible with life, but he's still functioning. It's as if the virus is keeping him operational despite catastrophic system failure."

Reyes collapsed to his knees, body convulsing violently now. A guttural sound escaped him—not quite a scream, not quite a growl, but something primal that raised the hair on the necks of everyone in the observation room. His fingers clawed at the floor, leaving deep gouges in the metal.

"Implement Code Black containment," Mercer ordered, voice tight with controlled fear as he activated the facility's most severe lockdown protocol. Metal shutters began to descend over the observation window, designed to seal the testing chamber completely.

The last thing Elara saw before the view was cut off was Reyes collapsing to the floor, blood pouring from his nose, eyes, and ears in thick rivulets. His body twisted unnaturally, joints bending in ways human anatomy shouldn't allow, as the virus rewrote him from the inside out. But worst was his expression—even through the mask of blood, she could see something like ecstasy on his face, a terrible pleasure in the transformation.

Then the shutters sealed with a final, ominous thud, leaving the observation room in silence broken only by the wail of alarms.

"Clear the room," Mercer ordered the observers, his military training taking over. "All non-essential personnel to emergency stations." As the military officials filed out, he turned to Elara and Jin, eyes hard. "You two, with me. I need to know exactly what we're dealing with, and how to stop it."

As they followed him out, Elara glanced back at the sealed shutters. They were designed to contain any biological threat, rated to withstand massive pressure and impact. She should have felt reassured by their solid presence.

Instead, she couldn't shake the feeling that no barrier they could build would be enough to contain what Reyes was becoming.

PART III
OUTBREAK

Four hours later, Reyes had been successfully contained—though he was no longer the man they'd known. The virus had ravaged his nervous system, leaving him in a state between conscious aggression and mindless rage. He was now in isolation, heavily sedated and restrained. The official position was that the trial had been a "partial success with unexpected side effects."

Elara sat in her lab, reviewing the test data with growing horror. The virus had worked exactly as designed in terms of physical enhancement, but the neurological impacts were far beyond anything they had modeled. Moreover, blood work showed that XV-27 was still active in Reyes's system, continually adapting and evolving.

"We've created a monster," Jin said quietly, looking over her shoulder at the readings.

"No," Elara corrected grimly. "We've created something worse. A monster is just a creature that frightens us. This... this is something that could fundamentally alter human biology without discrimination."

The lab door slid open. Colonel Mercer entered, flanked by two security officers. His face was a careful mask of control, but Elara could see the tension in his jaw.

"Status report," he demanded.

"R-9's physical enhancements are holding stable," she said, professional despite her misgivings. "Accelerated healing, enhanced strength and reflexes, all as designed. But the neurological effects are devastating. There's evidence of synaptic degradation, massive neurotransmitter imbalances, and complete breakdown of normal inhibitory functions."

"Explain," Mercer ordered.

Jin stepped in. "In layman's terms, the virus enhances the body but destroys the mind. It's creating a perfect killer with no restraint, no higher reasoning, just primal aggression and instinct."

"Can it be controlled?" Mercer asked.

Elara stared at him in disbelief. "That's your concern? Not that we've created something that can turn people into mindless killing machines?"

"My concern, Doctor, is the mission," Mercer replied coldly. "If this side effect can be harnessed—"

"It can't," Jin interrupted. "And worse, we have evidence the virus is becoming airborne. A technician who wasn't even in the testing chamber is showing early symptoms."

Mercer's face paled slightly. "Confirm that. Now."

A lab technician rushed in, face white with fear. "Dr. Voss, Dr. Takeda—you need to see this."

They followed him to the main monitoring station, where screens displayed various sections of the facility. The technician pointed to one showing the air filtration system. "We were running routine maintenance scans and found this."

The screen showed minuscule particles floating in the filtration chamber, glittering strangely under the sampling light.

"Is that...?" Jin began.

"XV-27," the technician confirmed. "It's in the air system. The virus has gone airborne."

Elara felt the floor drop away beneath her. "Containment breach. Full lockdown, now!"

The technician was already hitting the alarm. Throughout the facility, warning lights began to flash, and steel containment doors slid into place with pneumatic hisses. The automated announcement system activated: "Attention all personnel. Biohazard containment protocols are now in effect. This is not a drill. Proceed to your designated safety zones. Attention all personnel..."

As chaos erupted around them, Elara caught Jin's eye. In his face, she saw her own fear reflected back at her.

"It's beginning," she whispered.

PART IV
THE DESCENT

The observation room for Isolation Chamber 5 was cramped and sterile, dominated by the large one-way glass panel that offered a view of Subject R-9. Reyes lay strapped to a reinforced medical bed, intravenous lines feeding a cocktail of sedatives directly into his bloodstream. Despite the drugs, his eyes remained open—alert, tracking movement with predatory focus, pupils dilated to pinpoints. Occasional tremors wracked his body, and his skin had taken on a sickly pallor, blue veins prominent beneath the surface.

"He should be unconscious," Dr. Jin Takeda muttered, studying the readouts. "We're administering enough sedatives to put down an elephant."

Elara Voss nodded grimly. "XV-27 is altering his metabolism in real-time. Look at the enzyme activity." She pointed to a graph on one of the monitors, showing steadily rising lines. "His liver is processing the sedatives faster than we can administer them."

Across the room, Colonel Mercer watched with a mixture of concern and calculation. "The virus is adapting to protect its host," he observed. "Fascinating."

"Protecting isn't the word I'd use," Elara said sharply. "It's destroying him, piece by piece."

Three days had passed since the initial test and subsequent airborne contamination discovery. The entire facility had been locked down, all personnel confined to their respective sections. So far, XV-27 had been contained within the air filtration system of the research wing, but Elara knew it was only a matter of time before someone else showed symptoms.

As if reading her thoughts, Mercer said, "Any signs of infection among the staff?"

Jin shook his head. "Three confirmed cases besides Reyes. All were in or near the testing chamber during the incident. They're isolated in the medical wing, showing early symptoms—elevated temperature, increased aggression, reporting auditory hallucinations."

"And containment?" Mercer pressed.

"Holding for now," Jin replied. "The virus is spreading through the ventilation system, but the HEPA filters and UV treatment in the cross-sectional barriers are keeping it contained to the research wing."

"Then we have time," Mercer said decisively. "We need to understand exactly what's happening with R-9 and develop a treatment protocol."

Elara stared at him incredulously. "Treatment? Colonel, we have an uncontained, airborne pathogen that rewrites human neurochemistry, and test subjects who are showing signs of violent psychosis."

"Which is why we need to work faster," Mercer countered. "This is still a military asset with potential applications."

"It's a disaster," she shot back. "We need to focus on creating a vaccine or antiviral agent before more people are infected."

Their argument was interrupted by a wet, gurgling sound from the isolation chamber. All three turned toward the source. Reyes was convulsing against his restraints, foam and blood pouring from his mouth.

"Seizure," Jin said, moving quickly to the intercom. "Medical team to Isolation 5, stat!"

A medical team in full biohazard suits entered the chamber, working frantically to stabilize Reyes. They administered anticonvulsants, cleared his airways, monitored his vital signs. Eventually, the seizure subsided, leaving Reyes unconscious but alive.

"What caused that?" Mercer demanded.

Jin checked the monitoring equipment. "Brain activity spiked in the limbic system right before the seizure. The virus is concentrating in areas associated with aggression and primal emotional responses."

"Is he still... Reyes?" Elara asked quietly.

Jin hesitated. "Questionable. PET scans show massive reorganization of neural pathways. Higher reasoning centers are showing decreased activity while areas associated with aggression, fear, and basic survival instincts are hyperactive."

"So he's becoming what—an animal?" Mercer asked.

"Worse," Elara said. "A predator with human intelligence but no human restraint or morality. And if the virus spreads..."

The implications hung heavily in the air.

The contamination spread faster than anyone anticipated. By the end of the week, fifteen staff members showed symptoms. The progression followed a clear pattern: first came fever and increased aggression, followed by paranoia and hallucinations, then violent outbursts, and finally a kind of feral state where the infected attacked anyone nearby with inhuman strength and savagery.

"The virus targets the amygdala first," Jin explained during the emergency briefing. They sat in the main conference room, department heads and security personnel arranged around a long table. Mercer stood at the head, his posture rigid with contained tension.

"It hijacks the fear response," Jin continued, "creating a constant state of fight-or-flight. As it progresses, it erodes higher brain functions while enhancing primal instincts and physical capabilities. The end result is a human with the mind of a predator—all aggression, no restraint."

"And transmission?" Mercer asked.

Elara stepped in. "Definitely airborne now, possibly also transmission through bodily fluids. We've isolated the infected personnel in the medical wing, but the virus is spreading through the ventilation system despite our best containment efforts."

"Prognosis for the infected?" Mercer turned his cold gaze on her.

She hesitated. "Unknown long-term. Short-term, they become increasingly violent and unpredictable. The virus doesn't seem to kill them directly—it transforms them."

"Into weapons," Mercer said thoughtfully.

"Into victims," Elara corrected sharply. "Colonel, we need to focus on developing a treatment or vaccine, not on potential military applications."

Before Mercer could respond, the facility's alarm system blared to life. Red emergency lights began to strobe across the ceiling.

"Medical emergency in Isolation Ward C," announced the automated system. "Medical emergency in Isolation Ward C."

That was where the infected personnel were being held.

Mercer was on his feet instantly. "Security team with me. Dr. Voss, Dr. Takeda, you too. Everyone else, remain here."

They rushed through the corridors, the alarm continuing its relentless wail. Armed guards flanked them, weapons ready. When they reached Isolation Ward C, the scene that greeted them was chaos.

One of the technicians—Elara recognized him as Davis, a quiet man who had always been meticulous in his work—had somehow broken free of his restraints. He was convulsing on the floor, foam flecking his lips, veins standing out like dark ropes against his pallid skin. Two medical staff were attempting to restrain him, but despite his slender build, he was overpowering them with unnatural strength. His eyes were bloodshot and wild, pupils contracted to pinpoints.

"Hold him down!" the head physician shouted. "I need five cc's of—"

Davis broke free with a roar that sounded barely human. He lunged at the nearest doctor, fingers curled like claws. Before he could reach his target, security opened fire. Stun rounds hit Davis in the chest, the electrical charge designed to incapacitate without killing.

He staggered... then straightened, the barbs from the stun rounds still embedded in his flesh. Turned. Snarled—a feral sound that raised the hair on Elara's neck. Then he charged.

The security team switched to lethal rounds, the sound of gunfire deafening in the enclosed space. Davis jerked as bullets tore through him, but kept coming. It took multiple shots to finally drop him.

In the sudden silence that followed, Elara became aware of a wet, gurgling sound. She turned to see one of the other infected personnel—a woman named Patel—convulsing on her bed. Blood poured from her mouth, nose, and eyes, a thick, dark flood that didn't seem possible from a human body.

"Her system is rejecting the changes," Jin whispered in horror. "The virus is destroying her from inside."

Before anyone could react, Patel's body gave a final, violent spasm, then went still. The blood flow continued, pooling beneath the bed.

"The third patient?" Mercer demanded, seemingly unfazed by the carnage.

The head physician pointed to another isolation room. "Chen. Still in early stages. High fever, increased aggression, but we have him heavily sedated."

Mercer turned to Elara and Jin. "Explanations. Now."

"The virus is expressing differently depending on the host," Elara said, mind racing to make sense of what they'd just witnessed. "Davis showed the full transformation—enhanced strength, complete loss of higher reasoning, extreme aggression. Patel's system rejected the changes completely, causing massive hemorrhaging and organ failure."

"And Chen?"

Jin checked the monitor displaying Chen's vitals. "Early stages. The virus progresses at different rates in different hosts, possibly due to variations in individual biology."

Mercer processed this. "So we have one subject neutralized, one in transition, and one dead from rejection."

"And we have no idea how many others might be infected," Elara added quietly. "The air filtration system services the entire research wing."

"Implement full biohazard protocols," Mercer ordered. "I want everyone tested immediately. Any sign of infection, the individual is quarantined. And double the guard on all isolation chambers."

As they left the isolation ward, Elara lingered for a moment, looking back at the blood-soaked scene. She couldn't shake the feeling that they'd crossed a line from which there was no return. They weren't just dealing with a virus anymore, but something that transformed its hosts into killing machines with terrifying efficiency.

And it was spreading through the facility, airborne and lethal.

PART V
ZERO OPTION

The days that followed brought a steady deterioration of the situation. More personnel showed symptoms, though the progression varied wildly. Some transformed rapidly like Davis had, becoming violent predators that required immediate containment. Others suffered catastrophic rejection like Patel, their bodies literally destroying themselves from within. A third group remained in a state of limbo—feverish, aggressive, but still recognizably human.

Elara and Jin worked frantically to develop a vaccine or antiviral agent, testing countless compounds against samples of the virus. But XV-27 adapted to each attempt, rewriting itself faster than they could formulate countermeasures.

"It's like it's evolving in real-time," Jin said after another failed trial. They were in the high-security lab, surrounded by equipment and the relentless hum of air purifiers. Both wore full containment suits despite the negative pressure environment—a precaution that felt increasingly futile.

"Not evolving," Elara corrected, studying a simulation on her screen. "This is what it was designed to do—adapt to protect itself and spread. We just never anticipated how effectively it would achieve those goals."

"That's not possible," Jin objected. "We built in fail-safes, genetic dead-ends that should prevent this kind of adaptation."

"And it found workarounds," Elara said softly. "XV-27 isn't just a pathogen anymore. It's a perfect parasite, rewriting its host to serve its own propagation."

Jin sat back, the implications washing over him. "So how do we fight something that adapts to every countermeasure we develop?"

Elara was silent for a long moment. "We need to think beyond conventional approaches. The virus adapts to specific threats... but what if we created something that adapts faster? A counter-virus designed to target XV-27's replication mechanisms?"

"A viral predator," Jin mused, interest kindling in his tired eyes. "It could work. But we'd need to understand exactly how XV-27 modifies its own genome to evade our treatments."

When they approached Mercer with the proposal, he was surprisingly receptive. The situation had deteriorated to the point where even he recognized the threat outweighed any potential military applications.

"How long would development take?" he asked.

"Weeks, maybe months under normal circumstances," Elara admitted. "But we don't have that kind of time. If we focus all our resources, maybe a few days for a prototype."

Mercer nodded grimly. "The infection rate is accelerating. At current progression, we'll lose containment within the facility inside of a week."

"And then?" Jin asked.

"And then we implement fail-safe protocols." Mercer's expression hardened. "This site is equipped with a tactical nuclear device, Dr. Takeda. If containment fails, we sterilize the facility."

The blunt statement hung in the air between them.

"How many people are still uninfected?" Elara asked quietly.

"Sixty-seven, out of the original two hundred and twelve," Mercer replied. "Primarily administrative staff and security personnel in the upper levels, where the air systems are separate."

"And the rest?"

"Thirty-two deceased. Seventy-four showing symptoms at various stages. Thirty-nine in the final stage—complete transformation into what we're now classifying as 'Predators.'"

"And Reyes?" Jin asked.

"Patient zero," Mercer said grimly. "Still contained, but barely. He's... evolving beyond our capacity to measure or control."

Elara's breath fogged inside her containment helmet as she made her way through the now-deserted corridors of Level 3. This section had been completely overrun two days ago, its personnel either evacuated, infected, or dead. The emergency lighting cast everything in a bloody red glow, shadows stretching like grasping fingers along the walls.

She moved cautiously, a guard in a matching containment suit preceding her with a raised rifle. They had come for specific viral samples stored in a secure lab—samples she needed for her counter-virus work. It was a calculated risk, but one they couldn't avoid. The samples contained earlier iterations of XV-27, crucial for understanding its evolutionary pathway.

"Movement ahead," the guard whispered through his comm system. "Thirty meters, junction B."

Elara froze. Through the reinforced faceplate of her suit, she peered down the corridor. At first, she saw nothing but shadows. Then movement—a figure lurching awkwardly into view. It had once been human, perhaps even someone she knew. Now it was something else.

The infected moved with an unnatural gait, head tilted at an impossible angle, limbs twitching sporadically. Its skin was mottled with dark veins, eyes sunken and feral. Blood and foam caked its mouth and chin. It hadn't seen them yet, but it would soon—the Predators seemed to have enhanced senses, particularly smell and hearing.

"We need to go around," Elara whispered.

The guard shook his head. "No alternative route. We neutralize and proceed."

Before she could object, he raised his rifle and fired—a single shot that caught the infected in the shoulder. It staggered back, then straightened with a howl that chilled Elara's blood even through her suit. Rather than retreat, it charged, moving with that unsettling combination of jerkiness and speed that characterized the fully transformed.

The guard fired again, multiple rounds striking center mass. The infected stumbled but kept coming, driven by the virus's relentless programming to spread itself. Only when a shot pierced its brain did it finally collapse, twitching, to the floor.

"Clear," the guard announced, but his voice held no triumph. "We move quickly. That noise will attract others."

They hurried past the fallen Predator, Elara trying not to look at its face—trying not to wonder who it had been before the virus rewrote its existence. They reached the secure lab without further incident, and Elara quickly located and retrieved the samples she needed.

The return journey proved more harrowing. Drawn by the earlier gunfire, infected personnel converged on the area. The guard was forced to neutralize three more Predators, each engagement more dangerous than the last. By the time they reached the checkpoint leading back to the safe zone, Elara's suit was spattered with blood, and her hands shook uncontrollably.

Mercer was waiting at the decontamination chamber. "Did you get what you needed?"

Elara nodded, unable to speak until her breathing steadied. "Early samples, intact. Jin has already prepared the lab for development."

"Good," Mercer said. Then, with uncharacteristic solemnity: "We just lost Level 4 completely. Containment breach in three separate sectors. The virus is spreading faster than we can contain it."

"How long?" Elara asked, though she dreaded the answer.

"Before complete facility contamination? Forty-eight hours, maximum. The nuclear option is being prepared for remote detonation in seventy-two hours."

The implication was clear: she had two days to develop a counter-virus, or everyone in the facility would die—either from infection or incineration.

"I need to get to work," she said simply, heading for the lab where Jin waited.

For the next thirty-six hours, Elara and Jin worked without rest, stopping only when absolute biological necessity demanded it. They tested dozens of viral vectors against XV-27, searching for one that could penetrate its rapidly evolving defenses. Each failure brought them closer to the inevitable conclusion: traditional approaches would not work.

"We need to use its own adaptability against it," Elara said, staring at yet another failed simulation. "Create something that looks like a benign mutation but carries a kill switch."

"A Trojan horse," Jin agreed, his eyes red-rimmed from exhaustion. "But how do we get past its remarkable defense mechanisms?"

The answer came from an unexpected source. One of the few remaining medical staff, Dr. Chen, had been monitoring Reyes since the beginning. He contacted the lab with a startling observation: Reyes was no longer progressing like the other infected.

"His transformation has... stabilized," Chen reported via video link. "He's still violent, still shows all the signs of infection, but he's not deteriorating neurologically like the others. It's as if his system has reached some kind of equilibrium with the virus."

"Impossible," Jin said. "The virus is designed to continually push for enhancement."

"See for yourself," Chen countered, sending over the latest scans.

Elara studied them with growing excitement. "He's right. Reyes's system has developed antibodies that aren't neutralizing the virus but are containing it—preventing it from continuing its neurological rampage."

"Natural immunity?" Jin asked skeptically.

"Not natural," Elara replied, mind racing. "Engineered. Remember that Reyes was part of the Prometheus program before receiving XV-27. His system was already enhanced through conventional means, including a modified immune response."

"Which is now keeping the virus in check," Jin finished, hope kindling in his tired eyes. "If we can isolate those antibodies—"

"We can create a treatment," Elara said. "Not a cure, but something that could prevent further neurological degradation in those already infected, and potentially a vaccine for those who aren't."

It was a slim hope, but the only one they had. Mercer authorized an emergency procedure to extract blood and cerebrospinal fluid from Reyes—a dangerous proposition given his condition, but necessary.

The extraction team consisted of six security personnel in reinforced containment suits, two medical technicians, and Dr. Chen supervising. Elara watched via video feed as they entered Reyes's isolation chamber, where he was strapped to a reinforced medical bed.

Even heavily sedated, Reyes reacted to their presence. His eyes snapped open—bloodshot but unnervingly focused—and he began straining against his restraints. The reinforced straps creaked but held as the team approached cautiously.

"Administering additional sedative," one of the technicians announced, injecting a massive dose directly into Reyes's IV line.

For a moment, it seemed to work. Reyes's struggles weakened, his eyelids drooping. The team moved in quickly, preparing to extract the needed samples. Then, without warning, his eyes flew open again. With a strength that defied comprehension, he tore free of the restraint securing his right arm.

"Containment breach!" Chen shouted. "Fall back!"

But it was too late. Reyes's free hand shot out with impossible speed, grabbing the nearest security officer by the throat. Even through the reinforced suit, the pressure was enough to crush the man's trachea. As the officer collapsed, Reyes used the momentary chaos to tear loose his other restraints.

What followed was a slaughter. Moving with predatory grace despite months of confinement, Reyes tore through the extraction team. The reinforced suits offered little protection against his enhanced strength. Within moments, the isolation chamber had become a bloodbath.

Only Dr. Chen managed to escape, sealing the chamber doors behind him. But Reyes wasn't attempting to pursue. Instead, he methodically examined the fallen team members, as if searching for something. Finding a security keycard, he approached the chamber's internal control panel.

"He's overriding the lock!" Chen's panicked voice came through the video feed. "This isn't mindless aggression—he knows exactly what he's doing!"

Elara watched in horror as Reyes manipulated the control panel with deliberate precision. The isolation chamber doors slid open, and he stepped out into the corridor, head tilted as if sniffing the air. Then he turned directly toward the nearest camera, staring into it with predatory focus.

"He's loose," Elara whispered, her blood running cold. "And he's hunting."

PART VI
PATIENT ZERO

"Full facility lockdown," Mercer ordered, his voice steady despite the crisis unfolding on the monitors before them. "All personnel to secure zones immediately. Security teams to Level 2, full tactical response authorized."

The command center had become the last bastion of order in the crumbling facility. Screens displayed chaotic scenes from throughout Polaris—infected personnel breaking containment, security teams fighting losing battles in blood-soaked corridors, uninfected staff barricading themselves in whatever rooms they could secure.

And at the center of the storm moved Reyes, patient zero, the first and most dangerous of the infected. Unlike the others who attacked indiscriminately, Reyes moved with purpose, avoiding security checkpoints, disabling surveillance systems, methodically working his way upward through the facility's levels.

"He's heading for the surface," Elara realized. "He knows the way out."

"That's impossible," Mercer objected. "The infection damages higher cognitive functions."

"Not in Reyes," Jin said quietly. "Remember, his system developed a partial equilibrium with the virus. He's maintained some higher reasoning while gaining all the physical enhancements. The worst possible combination."

Mercer's face hardened. "Implement Protocol Zero. No one leaves this facility."

Protocol Zero—the last-resort option before nuclear sterilization. All exits would be permanently sealed, all emergency systems locked down. Everyone inside would be trapped, infected or not.

"We still need those samples from Reyes," Elara said urgently. "Without them, the counter-virus development can't proceed."

"You want us to capture him?" Mercer asked incredulously. "You saw what he did to a fully equipped extraction team."

"Not capture," Elara said grimly. "Just sample. We can try to retrieve blood from the isolation chamber or from injuries he's sustained. Partial samples are better than none."

Mercer considered this, then nodded to a security officer. "Team Alpha to the isolation chamber. Retrieve any viable biological samples and return immediately."

As the officer hurried to relay the orders, Jin leaned closer to Elara. "Even if we get the samples, we've lost nearly half our development time. The nuclear option is set for detonation in less than thirty-six hours."

"Then we work faster," she replied with determination she didn't entirely feel.

The biological samples retrieved from Reyes's isolation chamber were degraded but usable. Working at breakneck speed, Elara and Jin managed to isolate the antibodies that had allowed Reyes's system to reach equilibrium with XV-27. These became the foundation for a dual-purpose treatment: a serum that could potentially stabilize those in early stages of infection, and a vaccine for the uninfected.

"It's ready for testing," Elara announced twenty-eight hours later, holding up a vial of cloudy liquid. "Simulation models show 87% effectiveness in preventing further neurological degradation in early-stage infection, and 94% effectiveness as a preventative vaccine."

"But it won't cure those already transformed," Jin clarified. "The neurological damage is irreversible past a certain point."

Mercer studied the vial with guarded hope. "How quickly can we produce enough doses?"

"With the facilities and materials we have left? Maybe a hundred doses in the next six hours," Elara estimated. "Enough for the remaining uninfected personnel."

"And deployment?" Mercer pressed.

"Injection is most effective," Jin said. "But we've also developed an aerosol version that could be introduced through the air systems. Less effective but wider coverage."

Mercer nodded decisively. "Begin production immediately. Security will escort uninfected personnel here in groups for vaccination. Dr. Takeda, supervise the aerosol deployment through whatever functioning air systems remain."

As they prepared to implement this last-ditch effort, a new alert sounded. One of the few remaining security cameras had captured Reyes again—this time in the engineering section, accessed only by the highest clearance levels.

"What's he doing?" Elara asked, watching as Reyes methodically examined a series of control panels.

"The nuclear failsafe controls," Mercer realized, color draining from his face. "He's trying to disable the remote detonation system."

"How would he even know about that?" Jin asked.

"The virus doesn't just enhance physical abilities," Elara said slowly. "It heightens certain cognitive functions while degrading others. Pattern recognition, spatial awareness, predatory instinct—all amplified. He's figuring things out, adapting in ways we never anticipated."

They watched helplessly as Reyes manipulated the engineering controls with disturbing precision. After several minutes, warning messages flashed across the command center's main screen: FAILSAFE SYSTEM COMPROMISED. REMOTE DETONATION DISABLED.

"He's cut off the nuclear option," Mercer said grimly. "If the virus reaches the surface now..."

The implication hung in the air, too terrible to articulate fully. An airborne pathogen that turned humans into hyper-aggressive predators, unleashed upon an unsuspecting world. Millions infected within weeks, civilization collapsing under the weight of an invisible apocalypse.

"We still have the vaccine," Elara insisted. "And the treatment. If we can reach the surface, warn the outside world—"

"No one leaves," Mercer stated flatly. "Protocol Zero remains in effect. This virus dies here, with us if necessary."

"There has to be another way," Jin argued.

Mercer's expression turned calculating. "The facility's reactor. If we can't use the nuclear failsafe, we can overload the main power core. It won't be as effective as a tactical nuclear device, but the meltdown would sterilize most of the facility."

"And kill everyone inside," Elara said quietly.

"Everyone is already dead," Mercer replied, his voice eerily calm. "The only question is whether we take this abomination with us."

Before Elara could argue further, the command center's reinforced doors buckled under a tremendous impact. Again. And again. Metal screamed as claws or tools pried at the seams, creating gaps that widened with each assault.

"He's found us," Jin whispered.

"Security protocols, now!" Mercer ordered. The few remaining guards took up defensive positions, weapons trained on the failing doors.

Elara made a split-second decision. Grabbing the rack of vaccine vials and as many prepared syringes as she could carry, she turned to Jin. "The maintenance shaft behind the server racks. It leads to Level 1. Take these, get to the surface, warn someone."

"What about you?" Jin asked, already moving to help her.

"I'll create a diversion," she said, loading a single vial into an aerosol dispersal device. "This won't stop him, but it might slow him down."

Jin hesitated, then embraced her quickly. "I'll make sure they know. I'll make sure this wasn't for nothing."

As Jin disappeared into the maintenance shaft with the precious vaccines, Elara turned back to face the doors just as they finally gave way. Reyes stepped through the breach, blood-spattered and feral, yet moving with disturbing deliberation. Behind him came others—transformed personnel who had once been colleagues, now reduced to predatory husks driven by viral instinct.

The guards opened fire, cutting down the followers but barely slowing Reyes. He moved through the hail of bullets with uncanny agility, wounds healing almost as quickly as they formed. Within moments, he had closed the distance, tearing through the security team with brutal efficiency.

Mercer, to his credit, stood his ground. As Reyes approached, the colonel raised his sidearm and fired directly at the creature's head. The bullet grazed Reyes's temple, momentarily staggering him. It was the opening Elara needed.

She activated the aerosol device, filling the air between them with a fine mist of the experimental treatment. Reyes paused, head tilted in that predatory way, nostrils flaring as he detected the unfamiliar substance. For a brief moment, something like recognition flickered in his feral eyes—a momentary glimpse of the man he had once been.

Then it was gone, replaced by pure predatory rage. He lunged forward, faster than Elara could track. She felt a searing pain as claws raked across her abdomen, then she was flying through the air, crashing against a bank of monitors.

Through a haze of pain, she saw Mercer engaged in a losing battle with Reyes. The colonel fought with military precision, but against Reyes's virus-enhanced capabilities, he stood no chance. In seconds, Mercer was on the ground, Reyes's foot pressed against his throat.

"The reactor," Mercer gasped, looking directly at Elara. "Manual... override... in engineering." His hand moved to his chest pocket, retrieving a small device—the engineering master key.

With his last strength, Mercer threw the key toward Elara. It skittered across the floor, coming to rest near her outstretched hand. Reyes, seeing this, let out an inhuman howl and moved to intercept. But Elara was quicker, snatching the key and dragging herself toward the secondary exit.

She made it through the doorway just as Reyes reached her, slamming the emergency closure button. The reinforced door slammed down, catching Reyes's arm. Even with his enhanced strength and healing, the severed limb would slow him down—but not for long.

Clutching her bleeding abdomen, Elara staggered through service corridors toward engineering. She had one chance left to stop the virus from reaching the surface. One terrible, final option.

PART VII

ZERO SUM

Engineering Level was eerily quiet compared to the chaos that had engulfed the rest of the facility. Most of the staff had either evacuated to the upper levels or succumbed to infection days ago. The massive reactor chamber hummed with contained power, status lights blinking in steady green patterns across the control consoles.

Elara stumbled to the main terminal, leaving a trail of blood in her wake. The wound in her abdomen wasn't immediately fatal, but without medical attention, she wouldn't last long. Not that it mattered—if she succeeded, no one in the facility would survive anyway.

Her hands trembled as she inserted Mercer's master key into the console. The screen lit up with restricted options, including the one she sought: CORE CONTAINMENT OVERRIDE.

"Don't do it, Elara."

The voice startled her. She turned to find Jin standing in the doorway, a vaccine injector in one hand.

"Jin? You were supposed to escape, warn the outside—"

"I couldn't leave," he said simply, approaching her. "Not without you. And not without making sure."

"Making sure of what?" she asked, wincing as a fresh wave of pain washed over her.

"That this is really necessary." He gestured at the reactor controls. "Once you initiate the meltdown, there's no going back. Everyone dies."

"Everyone's already dead," Elara echoed Mercer's words. "You saw what the virus does. If it reaches the surface—"

"We have the vaccine," Jin countered. "And the treatment. I've already inoculated myself and set up aerosol dispersal in the remaining ventilation systems. It's working, Elara. The early-stage infected are stabilizing."

Hope flickered briefly in her chest, then died. "Stabilizing isn't cured. And what about the fully transformed? What about Reyes?"

Jin's expression fell. "No effect on advanced cases. But the stabilized cases aren't progressing further. It's something, at least."

Elara shook her head. "Not enough. The risk is too great." She turned back to the console. "This has to end here."

"Wait," Jin said urgently. He approached her, holding out the injector. "At least take the vaccine. In case... in case there's another way."

She hesitated, then allowed him to administer the injection. The serum burned as it entered her bloodstream, but it brought with it an odd clarity. For the first time in days, her mind felt sharp, focused.

"Thank you," she said quietly. "Now go. Try for the surface. Take whatever vaccine doses you can carry. Maybe someone will survive to tell the story."

Jin started to object, then nodded slowly. "How long?"

"Twenty minutes until meltdown becomes irreversible. Another fifteen before critical mass." She managed a weak smile. "Plenty of time to reach minimum safe distance."

They both knew it was a lie. No one would escape the facility in time, especially with the transformed hunting throughout the upper levels. But the fiction gave them comfort in these final moments.

Jin embraced her one last time, then turned to leave. At the doorway, he paused. "It wasn't your fault, you know. None of us could have predicted how the virus would adapt."

"But I designed it," Elara replied softly. "Whatever it's become, it started with me."

After Jin left, Elara turned back to the console and began the override sequence. Warnings flashed across the screen, requiring multiple confirmations—failsafes against accidental activation that now seemed almost quaint given the horror that had overtaken the facility.

FINAL AUTHORIZATION REQUIRED, the screen demanded.

Elara hesitated, her finger hovering over the confirmation button. Was she making the right choice? Was there truly no other option?

"Don't."

The voice froze her blood. Not Jin's voice this time, but something familiar yet distorted—a human voice filtered through an inhuman consciousness. She turned slowly.

Reyes stood in the doorway, or what Reyes had become. The wound where his arm had been severed was already healing, new tissue forming before her eyes. Blood covered his tattered clothing, none of it his own. His eyes burned with feral intelligence as he studied her.

"You know me," Elara said carefully, edging back toward the console. "You remember who I am."

"Doctor," Reyes responded, the word guttural but recognizable. "Creator."

"Yes," she confirmed, surprised by his apparent lucidity. "I created the virus that changed you."

Reyes tilted his head, that predatory gesture that had become so familiar and terrifying. "Not... changed. Improved."

"Is that what you think?" Elara asked, genuinely curious despite her fear. "That you're better now?"

"Stronger. Faster. Clearer." He took a step into the chamber. "Old thoughts... gone. Only instinct. Only now."

"And the others like you? The ones who died in pain, or lost their minds completely?"

A flicker of something crossed Reyes's face—perhaps confusion, perhaps regret. "Weak. Not... worthy."

"Natural selection," Elara murmured. "The virus is creating its own evolutionary pressure."

Reyes took another step toward her. "You... trying to stop evolution."

"I'm trying to stop extinction," she corrected. "Your kind would destroy humanity as we know it."

"Replace it," he countered. "Better version. Stronger. Adapted."

"A world of predators would collapse within a generation," Elara said. "You need prey to survive, but if everyone becomes like you, who will you hunt?"

This seemed to give him pause. For a moment, something almost human flickered in his eyes—doubt, perhaps, or the remnants of a consciousness not fully erased by the virus.

Elara seized the opportunity, lunging for the console. Her fingers pressed the confirmation button just as Reyes sprang forward with inhuman speed. Pain exploded across her back as his remaining hand tore through skin and muscle, but it was too late to stop the sequence.

CORE CONTAINMENT OVERRIDE INITIATED, the screen confirmed. MELTDOWN IN T-MINUS 19:57.

Reyes howled—a sound of pure rage that echoed through the engineering chamber. He grabbed Elara by the throat, lifting her from the ground with his one arm. Through the fog of pain and oxygen deprivation, she saw fury in his eyes, but also something else—fear. The predator sensed the approaching end.

"Too late," she gasped. "It's over."

"Fix it," he snarled, shaking her violently. "Stop it!"

"I can't," she managed, darkness creeping at the edges of her vision. "No one can."

With a roar of frustration, Reyes threw her across the room. She struck a support pillar with bone-crushing force and crumpled to the floor, unable to move. Through blurred vision, she watched as Reyes attacked the console, trying to halt the meltdown sequence. But the system was designed to prevent such interventions—once initiated, the override could not be stopped without external authorization.

Realizing the futility of his efforts, Reyes turned back to Elara, his expression a disturbing mixture of rage and calculation. He crossed to where she lay and crouched beside her.

"You die," he growled. "We all die. No escape."

"No escape," she agreed, tasting blood in her mouth. "The virus ends here."

Reyes studied her for a long moment, head tilted in that characteristic predatory assessment. Then, to her surprise, he sat back on his haunches, almost thoughtful.

"Virus... adapt," he said slowly. "Always adapt."

A chill that had nothing to do with her injuries ran through Elara. "What do you mean?"

Instead of answering directly, Reyes reached out with his remaining hand and touched her face with unexpected gentleness. "You... infected."

Horror dawned as Elara realized the implication. When his claws had torn through her back, her blood had mingled with his. Direct fluid transmission—the most efficient vector for XV-27.

"No," she whispered. "I took the vaccine."

"Vaccine... for old virus." Reyes's lips curled in what might have been a smile on a human face. "I am... new virus."

The burning sensation she had attributed to her injuries suddenly took on new significance. It was spreading through her system, an unnatural heat that radiated outward from the wound. The vaccine might slow the progression, but against Reyes's evolved strain, it wouldn't stop it completely.

"How long?" she asked, already knowing the answer.

"Not long," Reyes confirmed. "Change comes. Before the fire."

He stood and moved toward the exit, apparently satisfied with this final victory. At the doorway, he paused and looked back at her.

"Evolution... finds a way," he said, in a moment of disturbing clarity. Then he was gone, heading upward toward the surface levels, leaving Elara alone with the countdown and the virus burning through her veins.

She tried to move, to pursue him, but her body wouldn't respond properly. Whether from her injuries or the advancing infection, she was effectively paralyzed from the waist down. All she could do was watch the countdown timer on the reactor console as it ticked inexorably toward zero.

17:22... 17:21... 17:20...

The burning sensation intensified, spreading up her spine and into her brain. With it came flashes of sensory information so vivid they were almost hallucinatory—the hum of the reactor suddenly deafening, the sterile scent of the engineering level overlaid with the copper tang of blood, her own and others'. The lights seemed brighter, colors more intense.

The virus was rewriting her neural pathways, enhancing some senses while degrading others. She could feel her higher reasoning beginning to fragment, primitive instincts surging to the forefront. Fear, hunger, rage—emotions in their rawest form threatened to overwhelm rational thought.

Yet the vaccine was having some effect. Unlike the others who had succumbed completely, Elara retained a core of self-awareness. She could feel the virus's influence, but she wasn't lost to it—not yet.

15:45... 15:44... 15:43...

With tremendous effort, she dragged herself to a nearby emergency terminal. The facility's surveillance system was still partially operational. She could track Reyes's progress as he moved upward through the levels, dispatching the few remaining security personnel who tried to stop him.

He was heading for the surface, for freedom. If he escaped before the meltdown, if he reached civilization...

Elara pulled herself upright, using the terminal for support. Pain screamed through her broken body, but the virus was already working on her injuries, knitting tissue and bone with unnatural speed. She could feel strength returning to her limbs, accompanied by that same burning sensation as her cells were rewritten.

She accessed the facility's few remaining operational systems. Most were locked down under Protocol Zero, but one option remained: the emergency evacuation protocol could be manually overridden from engineering. Designed as a last-resort measure to save personnel in case of imminent disaster, it would open all remaining evacuation routes.

Including the surface access points.

Elara hesitated, her finger hovering over the activation command. What she was considering was tactically sound but morally reprehensible. Opening the evacuation routes would allow any surviving uninfected personnel a chance to escape the coming meltdown.

It would also create a clear path for Reyes—and any other transformed individuals—to reach the surface.

12:17... 12:16... 12:15...

The virus continued its assault on her system, making it increasingly difficult to focus on complex moral calculations.

Predatory instinct whispered that survival was the only imperative that mattered. Yet something else—perhaps the vaccine, perhaps her own stubborn humanity—insisted there were principles worth dying for.

She made her decision.

Instead of activating the evacuation protocol, Elara accessed the facility's communication system. Most external channels were severed under Protocol Zero, but the emergency beacon remained operational—designed to broadcast a simple distress signal with minimal data.

Elara modified the beacon, uploading all the data she could access: the virus's structure, its transmission vectors, the vaccine formulation, and a warning about Reyes. If anyone survived to retrieve the data, they would at least have a fighting chance against what was coming.

10:03... 10:02... 10:01...

With that task complete, she turned her attention to tracking Reyes. He had reached Level 1, encountering unexpected resistance from a group of security personnel who had barricaded themselves near the main surface access point. The ensuing battle was buying precious time, but Elara knew it wouldn't be enough. Reyes would eventually break through, and the meltdown was still minutes away.

There was one last option. Emergency Bulkhead Protocol—designed to compartmentalize the facility in case of structural failure. If activated from engineering, it would seal all major junctions, including the surface access points. No one would get out—but more importantly, nothing would get in after the meltdown.

It wasn't a perfect solution. The bulkheads weren't designed to withstand a full reactor meltdown, and there was no guarantee they would remain intact. But they would add another layer of containment, another obstacle between the virus and the outside world.

Elara activated the protocol. Throughout the facility, massive steel bulkheads slammed into place, sealing off each section. On the surveillance feed, she saw Reyes's head snap up as he heard the distant sound of machinery. Understanding dawned in his feral eyes. He abandoned his attack on the security team and sprinted toward the nearest surface access, but it was too late. The bulkhead descended before he could reach it.

7:22... 7:21... 7:20...

The virus's grip on Elara's mind tightened, rationality flickering like a candle in a strong wind. She found herself pacing the engineering level, movements becoming more predatory with each circuit. Part of her—a growing part—wanted to find a way out, to hunt, to spread what was inside her.

But the core of her identity held firm, anchored by the knowledge of what she had done and what was coming. This was her responsibility, her burden to bear. The virus had begun with her, and it would end with her.

5:10... 5:09... 5:08...

On the surveillance feeds, chaos reigned. Reyes had abandoned subtlety for brute force, tearing at the sealed bulkhead with inhuman strength. Other infected individuals joined him, acting with disturbing coordination despite their feral state. They were making progress—the bulkhead designed to withstand structural pressure, not sustained assault from within.

Elara realized with grim clarity that the meltdown might not be enough. If Reyes and the others breached the surface access before the reactor reached critical mass...

There was one final option, one last terrible choice. The facility's self-destruct system—separate from the reactor, designed as an absolute last resort. It would trigger explosive charges placed at strategic structural points, collapsing the entire facility instantly. Nothing would survive, infected or not.

The system required authorization from the facility commander—Mercer, now dead at Reyes's hands. But Elara had accessed enough emergency protocols that the system might recognize her credentials in the absence of higher authority.

3:45... 3:44... 3:43...

She accessed the self-destruct terminal, expecting to be denied. To her surprise, the system accepted her emergency override. WARNING: SELF-DESTRUCT SEQUENCE REQUIRES SECONDARY CONFIRMATION, the screen advised. PROCEED?

On the surveillance feed, Reyes and the others had created a sizeable gap in the bulkhead. It wouldn't hold much longer.

Elara's fingers hovered over the confirmation button. The virus raged through her system, her thoughts becoming increasingly fragmented. But her purpose remained clear—the infection must be contained, regardless of cost.

She pressed the button.

SELF-DESTRUCT SEQUENCE INITIATED. T-MINUS 60 SECONDS. EVACUATION ADVISED.

The bitter irony of that last automated line wasn't lost on Elara. There would be no evacuation, no escape. That was the entire point.

On the surveillance feed, Reyes suddenly stopped his assault on the bulkhead. He turned toward the nearest camera, as if sensing what she had done. For a brief moment, their eyes met across the digital divide—predator to predator, creator to creation.

Then the feed went dark as emergency power rerouted to critical systems.

Elara sank to the floor, her back against the cold wall of the engineering level. The virus's fire burned through her veins, rewriting her very being with each passing second. Yet in these final moments, her mind achieved a strange clarity.

She had created something terrible, something that could have ended humanity as they knew it. But she would also end it, here and now, before it could spread beyond these Arctic walls.

The countdown reached zero.

In the frozen wasteland above, nothing marked the passing of Research Station Polaris except a brief tremor in the ice, quickly swallowed by the howling Arctic wind. The explosion was contained entirely underground, leaving only a slight depression in the endless white landscape.

Six months later, a routine monitoring flight reported an anomalous radiation signature from the area. An investigation team found only fragments of debris scattered across the ice—insufficient to determine what had occurred there.

But buried deep in the ice, protected by specialized shielding, a small beacon continued its silent broadcast. A warning about what had been created and what might come again. A record of humanity's ambition and its consequences. And a formulation for a vaccine—incomplete but promising—should history repeat itself.

Because in the endless dance of evolution, adaptation is inevitable.

And something had survived.

EPILOGUE
EMERGENCE

THREE MONTHS LATER - BARROW, ALASKA

Dr. Malcolm Reid hunched against the Arctic wind as he left the small clinic, his medical bag clutched tightly in gloved hands. The northern lights shimmered overhead, casting an eerie green glow across the snow-covered town. He'd been called to examine a patient with unusual symptoms—high fever, increased aggression, strange neurological anomalies. The third such case this week.

His satellite phone buzzed. It was Dr. Amira Kwan from the CDC field office they'd hastily established two weeks ago.

"Malcolm, we've got the results from those blood samples," she said, her voice tight with tension. "You need to see this now."

Twenty minutes later, he stood in stunned silence, staring at the molecular imaging on Amira's laptop screen.

"It's unlike anything I've ever seen," she said quietly. "The viral structure keeps changing every time we try to isolate it. And look at these protein markers—they're almost... engineered."

"Not almost," Malcolm replied grimly. "Definitely engineered. This isn't natural evolution."

"What are you saying?"

Malcolm hesitated. "Six months ago, a research facility went dark about two hundred miles north of here. Military involvement, classified project. The official story was a reactor malfunction."

"You think this came from there?" Amira asked.

"I think something survived that wasn't supposed to."

TWO WEEKS LATER - ANCHORAGE, ALASKA

The quarantine wasn't holding. Despite the National Guard blockades and the CDC's best efforts, cases were appearing throughout Anchorage. The pattern was becoming clear—initial infection presented like a severe flu, followed by neurological symptoms, culminating in either violent psychosis or complete system failure.

Most disturbing was the variability. Some victims succumbed within days, while others developed a strange equilibrium with the virus, maintaining cognitive function while exhibiting enhanced physical abilities and extreme predatory behavior.

General Xavier Harwick—the same man who had once pressured Colonel Mercer for results from Project Prometheus—now found himself coordinating the military response to its escaped creation. In a secure bunker beneath Joint Base Elmendorf-Richardson, he reviewed the latest reports with mounting dread.

"Confirmed cases in Seattle and Vancouver," his aide reported. "And unconfirmed reports from Chicago and Toronto. It's spreading faster than our models predicted."

"Air travel," Harwick muttered. "We were too slow with the travel restrictions."

"Sir, there's something else. The beacon we recovered from the Polaris site—the tech team finally decoded part of its data package."

The aide handed him a tablet. Among schematics and partial formulas was a single video file. Harwick played it, coming face to face with a woman he recognized from the Polaris personnel files—Dr. Elara Voss, the lead virologist.

In the recording, her face was gaunt, skin mottled with dark veins. But her eyes remained clear, focused with terrible purpose.

"My name is Dr. Elara Voss. If you're seeing this, then XV-27 has escaped containment. The virus was designed as a temporary immune system modifier, but it has evolved far beyond its original parameters. It adapts to every countermeasure, learns from every host, becomes more efficient with each transmission."

She paused, fighting some internal battle before continuing.

"I've included formulas for a vaccine based on antibodies from Patient Zero—a partially immune host. The vaccine won't cure advanced cases, but it can prevent infection and stabilize early progression. It's incomplete—we ran out of time—but it's a starting point."

The recording ended with a final warning: "The virus is always adapting. Whatever you develop, it will eventually overcome. You must stay ahead of it. Good luck."

Harwick set down the tablet, a cold certainty settling in his stomach. They weren't containing this. The best they could hope for was to manage the inevitable.

As he turned to issue new orders, his aide burst back into the room, face pale with shock.

"Sir, we've lost contact with the Seattle quarantine zone. Complete communications blackout."

"Equipment failure?" Harwick asked, already knowing the answer.

"No, sir. The last transmission reported coordinated attacks on the perimeter. Not random assaults—tactical strikes at strategic points. The infected are... organizing."

ONE MONTH LATER - UNDISCLOSED LOCATION

Dr. Jin Takeda examined his reflection in the small mirror of his makeshift lab. The dark veins beneath his skin had stabilized, no longer spreading but not receding either. His eyes were clearer than they had been in weeks, the feverish gleam replaced by something else—a predatory sharpness that both disturbed and fascinated him.

He had survived the destruction of Polaris, escaping just before the self-destruct sequence initiated. The experimental vaccine Elara had administered in those final moments had kept the virus from completely overwhelming his system. He wasn't fully transformed, not like Reyes had been. But he wasn't fully human anymore either.

The blood sample under his microscope told the story. XV-27 had integrated with his cellular structure, rewriting portions of his DNA while leaving others intact. He was something new—a hybrid. And he wasn't alone.

Reports were scattered and unreliable, but the pattern was emerging. Across the infection zones, a small percentage of victims—perhaps one in a hundred—achieved this same equilibrium. Not mindless predators, not unaltered humans, but something in between. Adapted.

Jin's satellite phone rang—a secure line, known to only a handful of people.

"We need you in Geneva," said a voice he recognized as belonging to the WHO Director of Emergency Response. "The vaccine formulations from your data are showing promise, but we need your expertise. A military transport is already en route to your location."

Jin hesitated, his enhanced senses detecting a subtle undertone in the man's voice. Fear. Not just of the virus, but of him.

"I'll be ready," he replied noncommittally.

He ended the call and returned to his research notes. The truth was, he wasn't sure he wanted to go. Something was happening to those like him—the Adapted, as he'd begun to think of them. The virus wasn't just changing their bodies; it was altering their perceptions, their instincts, perhaps even their loyalties.

Last night, he'd dreamed of Elara in those final moments at Polaris. In reality, he'd left her behind to complete the containment protocols. But in the dream, she had survived, changed like him. And she had spoken words that still echoed in his mind:

"We aren't the enemy of humanity, Jin. We're its future."

A knock at his door interrupted his thoughts. Instead of the military escort he expected, he found a woman he'd never seen before. Her skin bore the same mottled pattern as his own, her eyes the same predatory sharpness.

"Dr. Takeda," she said, voice calm but urgent. "There are others like us. We need your help."

"Who are you?" Jin asked, already knowing the answer on some deeper level.

"My name is Maya. I was a virologist at the CDC before I was infected." She glanced nervously over her shoulder. "The military transport coming for you—it's not taking you to Geneva. There's a new facility, purpose-built for studying people like us. They call it 'containment,' but it's vivisection."

Jin felt a chill that had nothing to do with the virus. "How do you know this?"

"Because I escaped from it." She pushed up her sleeve, revealing a series of surgical scars. "They're afraid of what we're becoming. And maybe they should be."

Jin thought of Elara's warning on the beacon: The virus is always adapting. Whatever you develop, it will eventually overcome.

"There's something else," Maya continued. "Something you need to see. We found Patient Zero."

"Reyes?" Jin asked, stunned. "He survived Polaris?"

"Not just survived," Maya replied, her expression unreadable. "Evolved. And he's gathering the Adapted together for something big. He sent me to find you."

Jin hesitated on the threshold of his cabin, caught between two worlds. Behind him lay his research, his attempt to help humanity fight the virus. Ahead lay answers about what he himself was becoming.

"The military transport will be here in an hour," he said finally. "We should be gone before then."

As they disappeared into the wilderness, satellites tracked their movement. In command centers across the globe, officials watched with growing alarm as similar patterns emerged worldwide—the Adapted finding each other, gathering in remote locations, forming communities beyond human control.

And somewhere in the shadow of Polaris's destruction, something stirred in the Arctic ice. Not just a viral remnant, but a consciousness—distributed across hosts, learning, adapting, evolving toward something no one had anticipated.

Something Elara had glimpsed in her final moments, as the virus rewrote her from within.

Something that whispered with her voice: Evolution finds a way.

TO BE CONTINUED

Enjoyed this book?

Share your thoughts with a review and help more readers discover it! Your feedback truly makes a difference.

To be the first to read my next book or for any suggestions about new translations, visit: https://arielsandersbooks.com/

SPECIAL BONUS

*Want this Bonus Ebook for **free**?*

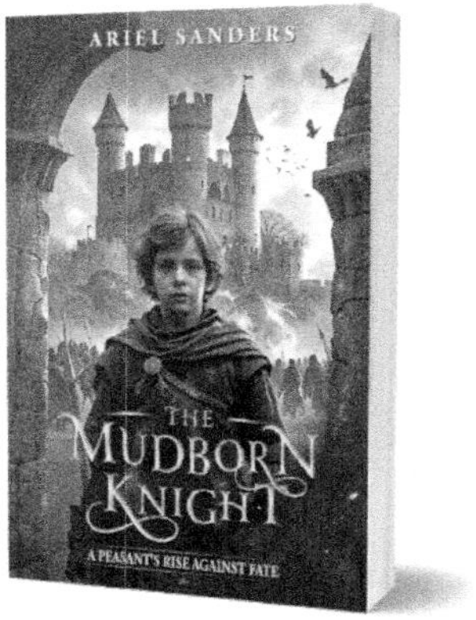

SCAN ME

SCAN W/ YOUR CAMERA TO DOWNLOAD THE EBOOK!

Printed in Dunstable, United Kingdom

64869872R00048